# Anansi's Narrow Waist

## A Tale from Ghana

H. J. Arrington

Illustrated by Nicole Allin

PELICAN PUBLISHING COMPANY
GRETNA 2016

*The word "Pelican" and the depiction of a pelican are
trademarks of Pelican Publishing Company, Inc., and are
registered in the U.S. Patent and Trademark Office.*

ISBN 9781455622160
E-book ISBN 9781455622177

Printed in Malaysia
Published by Pelican Publishing Company, Inc.
1000 Burmaster Street, Gretna, Louisiana 70053

Time was, in Ghana-land, folks say all spiders were as round as the sun. Now Anansi (pronounced Ah-nahn-see) the spider was thought to be the roundest of all. Maybe it was because he was the greediest fellow in town. Anansi loved to eat more than anything else in the world.

Not only was he greedy, but he was also known to be very clever. Anansi spent most of his time trying to get his next meal through trickery. Maybe he was the laziest fellow in town. He was certainly one of the cleverest.

One fine day, Anansi woke very early and felt mighty hungry. He rubbed his big belly as he hunted through his house for food. Finding none, he set out to find something delicious to eat.

He went walking, walking, walking. Woo! Suddenly, his nose started to twitch. "Hmm," Anansi mumbled to himself. "Where is that sweet smell coming from?"

He followed his nose for a bit.

"Oh! I smell yams cooking!" Anansi screeched loudly with delight! "I LOVE yams!"

As he came upon a clearing in the small village, he spied a few folks huddled around an open fire pit. They were roasting yams.

"Welcome Friend Spider," they called out as was the custom in that part of Africa.

"I smelled the yams cooking. Oh they smell so-o-o good!"

"And I'm sure they will be tasty when they are done. Why don't you join us in preparing our feast and you can eat with us?"

Now this sounded like work to Anansi and he did not want to work. All he wanted to do was eat.

He got an idea.

"I would love to help but I have a great errand to run. Then I will return to eat." He handed one end of a web string from around his big old belly and said, "Just pull on this string when the food is done and I will return to feast with you."

The villagers agreed and off scampered Anansi with a huge grin on his face.

"Oh—I'm gon eat good today. Yes. Oh—I'm gon to eat good." What a clever fellow! He'd get to eat and not work a bit! He went walking, walking, walking. Woo!

Suddenly, his nose twitched once more. "Hmm," Anansi mumbled to himself. "Where is that sweet smell coming from?" He followed his nose for a bit. "Oh! I smell chicken and rice cooking!" Anansi shouted loudly with delight! "I LOVE chicken and rice!"

As he came upon a clearing in the small village, he spied a few folks huddled around a huge earthenware pot. They were stirring the yummy stew.

"Welcome Friend Spider," they called out as was the custom in that part of the world.

"I smelled the chicken and rice stew cooking. Oh it smells so-o-o good!"

"And I'm sure it will be tasty when it is done. Why don't you join us in preparing our feast and you can eat with us?"
Now this sounded like work to Anansi and he did not want to work. All he wanted to do was eat. So he told the same tale.

"I would love to help but I have a great errand to run. But I will return to eat." He handed one end of a web string from round his big old belly and said, "Just pull on this string when the food is done and I will return to feast with you."

The villagers agreed and off scampered Anansi with a huge grin on his face.

"Oh–I'm gon eat good today. Yes. Oh–I'm gon to eat good." What a clever fellow! He'd get to eat and not work a bit!

He went walking, walking, walking. Woo! Suddenly, his nose twitched yet again. "Hmm," Anansi mumbled to himself. "Where is that sweet smell coming from?" He followed his nose for a bit. "Oh! I smell beans cooking!" Anansi giggled loudly with delight! "I LOVE beans!"

As he moved toward a clearing in the small village, he noticed a few folks crowded around a gigantic iron kettle. They were cooking beans.

"Welcome Friend Spider," they called out as was their custom.

"I smelled the beans cooking. Oh they smell so-o-o good!"

"And I'm sure they will be tasty when they are done. Why don't you join us in preparing our feast and you can eat with us?"

Now this sounded like work to Anansi and he did not want to work. All he wanted to do was eat. He told the same tale.

"I would love to help but I have a great errand to run. But I will return to eat." He handed one end of a web string from round his big old belly and said, "Just pull on this string when the food is done and I will return to feast with you."

The villagers agreed and off scampered Anansi with a huge grin on his face.

"Oh–I'm gon eat good today. Yes. Oh–I'm gon to eat good." What a clever fellow! He'd get to eat and not work a bit!

Anansi spent the rest of the morning
visiting from village to village.
He went walking, walking, walking. Woo!

Every time he found food, Anansi left another one of his web strings for the people to pull when the meal was ready to eat. Anansi was so pleased with himself. He would get to eat all afternoon and without doing one ounce of work!

Anansi walked and dreamed about all the delicious food he would soon be eating. Suddenly, he felt a tug on one of his web strings. It came from the village to the east.

"Yummy!" Anansi smiled. "Those tasty yams are ready." He started to scurry eastward.

Just then he felt another web string being tugged. This time it came from the west.

"Oh, no! The chicken and rice stew is also ready!" cried Anansi.

And then came a tug from the north. "The beans are ready!"

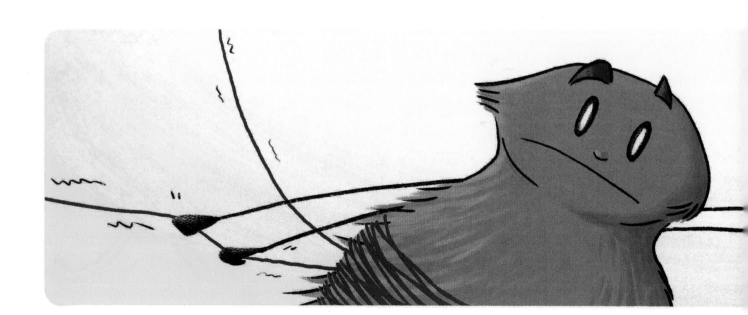

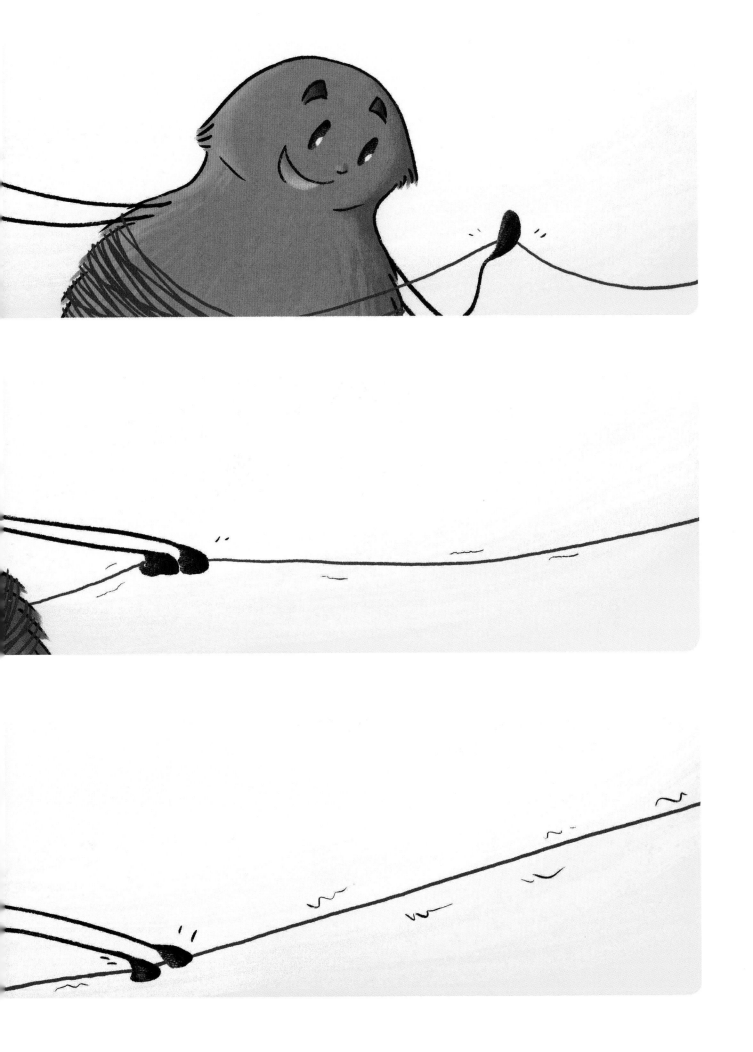

More and more tugs! Anansi was pulled from the east, the west, the north and the south-all at once.

Each feast seemed to be ready at the same time!

Anansi could not move. He was pulled and pulled from every direction.

His belly was being squeezed! And right before his eyes, his huge waist became smaller and smaller. Each pull on a web string squeezed his belly more and more.

Anansi wiggled and squirmed but that only made the web strings tighter.

His waist grew smaller.
And smaller.
And smaller.
And smaller.

And that my friends, is how the spider got his narrow waist. That was then and this is now. Even today, all spiders still carry the narrow waist of greedy Anansi!

*"The pleasure of greed is often outweighed by the pain it brings."*
—Ghanaian Proverb

# Anansi Approved Recipes

## Village Baked Beans

### Ingredients:
6 to 8 strips bacon, cut in 1-inch pieces
3 cans (16 ounces each) baked pork and beans
¼ cup light brown sugar, packed
½ teaspoon dry mustard
½ cup ketchup, or use part barbecue sauce

### Preparation:
Fry bacon until crisp; drain well on paper towels. Combine all ingredients; transfer to crockpot; cover and cook on low for 4 to 5 hours. Stir occasionally.
Serves 6 to 8.

---

## Classic Candied Yams with Marshmallows

### Ingredients:
3 medium yams or sweet potatoes (1 pound)
3 tablespoons brown sugar
1 tablespoon butter or margarine
¼ to ½ cup tiny marshmallows

### Preparation:
Place the yams in a large saucepan; cover with water. Boil for 25 to 35 minutes or until the yams are tender. Drain the yams and let them stand until cool enough to handle. Peel the yams, then cut into ½-inch-thick slices. Place half the yams in a 1-quart casserole dish. Layer with half the brown sugar and half the margarine. Repeat the layers. Bake, uncovered, in a 375 degree F. oven for 30 to 35 minutes or until the yams are glazed, spooning the liquid over the yams once or twice during cooking. Sprinkle with marshmallows and bake for 5 minutes more.
Serves 4-6.

# Author's Note

Stories of Anansi (pronounced Ah-nahn-see) are some of the best known in the folklore of West Africa. Anansi the spider is a character thought to originate with the Ashanti people, a tribe from Ghana in West Africa. He is popular in West African folklore and also in Caribbean folklore. Anansi is also known as Ananse, Kwaku Ananse, and Anancy.

Anansi is first and foremost considered to be a master at the art of trickery. Whether he is depicted in the image of an ordinary spider or as one with human characteristics, Anansi remains to be quite a remarkable fellow.

There are hundreds of Anansi tales, including many variations of the same basic storyline. Like tricksters from other cultures, Anansi is known to be clever, greedy, mischievous, and even foolish. Whether he is being wise or lazy, there is always a lesson about human nature to be learned in these stories.

In some tales, Anansi emerges as a strong and wise godlike persona who is widely respected. He is seen as the keeper of wisdom; therefore, much can be learned from him. In other stories, he is primarily a foolish, greedy or lazy character whose antics often get him into trouble. The overriding theme to all Anansi stories is one of learning from our actions and behaviors. They are fun to read, to share and to act out. Anansi can always make us smile, think critically, and see ourselves and others through his engaging adventures in life.

–H. J. Arrington
HarrietteArrington@msn.com